Fireman

AND THE BIRTHDAY CAKE

by Alison Boyle

Illustrations by The County Studio

HEINEMANN · LONDON

Dilys Price, Norman's mum, was busy cooking for Norman's birthday party.

"It's going to be magic!" said Norman, putting some
crackers on the table. "Fireman Sam is going to come, too."

"I wonder where the cake is?" thought Norman, looking in all the cupboards.

His mother watched him through the door. "You won't find it in there," she laughed.

James and Sarah arrived. "Happy birthday, Norman!" they called, giving him their birthday presents.

"Thanks, you two. These are really great," said Norman as
he unwrapped a drum and a whistle.

"Look at me! I'm a one-man-band!" cried Norman and he marched round the room.

"Norman, off you go upstairs, while I get your surprise ready," called Dilys. Norman marched up the stairs.

Trevor Evans and Fireman Elvis Cridlington were the next to arrive. "Fireman Sam is very sorry, but he can't come. He's still on duty," said Elvis.

"Where's Bella?" asked Trevor, looking around.
"Ssh, it's a surprise," said Sarah, as Bella peeped round the front door.

"Come down now, Norman," called Dilys, turning out the lights.

"Happy Birthday to you," sang Bella, coming in with a birthday cake.

Norman marched down the stairs whistling and drumming.
"Toot! Toot! Bang! Bang! Bang!"

"Mamma mia!" shrieked Bella. "What a terrible noise," and she jumped out of the way.

The birthday cake crashed to the floor. The burning candles set alight the wrapping paper that was lying on the floor.

Trevor threw his coat over the flames to put them out. "Quick, outside everyone," called Elvis, helping James and Sarah through the door.

Everyone waited outside while Elvis called the fire brigade from the call box.

A few minutes later Fireman Sam and Station Officer Steele arrived in Jupiter.

Fireman Sam ran inside and put out the flames.
"It's all right now," he called.

"What about my birthday cake," cried Norman looking at
the mess on the floor. The cake was ruined.

"Why don't you all come over to the cafe?" asked Bella. "I've
got one of my special ice cream cakes in the freezer."

"That sounds like a really good idea," smiled Fireman Sam.
"We'll clear up here and then all go to the cafe."

Norman blew out the candles on the ice cream cake.
"Well, at least the fire meant you had to come to my party,
Fireman Sam!" he laughed.